Beside The Sea

For F.M.B

First published in Great Britain by
HarperCollins Publishers Ltd in 1994
First published in Picture Lions in 1995
Picture Lions is an imprint of the Children's Division,
part of HarperCollins Publishers Ltd
Copyright © Mark Burgess 1994
A CIP catalogue record for this title
is available from the British Library.
The author asserts the moral right
to be identified as the author of the work.
ISBN: 0 00 664546 1
Printed and bound in Hong Kong

HANNAH'S HOTEL

Beside The Sea

MARK BURGESS

PictureLions

An Imprint of HarperCollinsPublishers

INTRODUCTION

A few years ago Hannah Hedgehog took over the little hotel by the sea from her Aunt Hetty. Hannah's aunt was tired of hotel life and had decided to travel the world in her hot air balloon.

These days Hannah's Hotel is the ideal place for a holiday. Hannah is helped by Molly Mouse; Sam Squirrel is the cook and Rodney Rabbit does all the odd jobs.

Everything is done to make the visitors happy. However, sometimes things don't go quite according to plan - such as the time Geraldine and Gillian Goose came to stay.

Hannah's Hotel is always busy.
Last Saturday was no exception.
A family of fifteen fieldmice had just left and
there was a lot of clearing up to do. Hannah
and Molly were hard at it.

"Ice-cream on the pillows again!" said Hannah.
"And it's chocolate.
Seems such a waste.
I wonder if Sam
could do
something
with it..."

"At least those fieldmice weren't as bad as the gerbils," said Molly.
"Oh, don't mention the gerbils! I never want to see another gerbil. I put notices in all the bedrooms but they still chewed the bedding. One mattress disappeared completely."

"Somebody is driving across the sand again," said Molly.
"Oh," said Hannah crossly, "some people never read notices."

The two geese parked their car in front of the hotel. Hannah came downstairs to meet them. "Hello," said Geraldine Goose. "We drove across, didn't we Gillian, dear?"
"Yes dear," said Gillian. "We saw the notice saying 'Do not drive across' but we thought it couldn't mean us."

"It's in case people get stuck in the soft sand when the tide's coming in," explained Hannah but the geese weren't listening. They were looking about, peering behind the pot plants and under the tables.

"What a nice hotel," said Geraldine. "I think we'll stay, shan't we Gillian, dear?"
"Ooo yes, of course we shall. Such a nice hotel."
Gillian prodded a cushion with her umbrella.

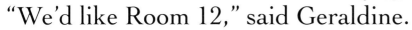

"We'd like Room 12," said Geraldine.
"We heard that Room 12 has a lovely view."

"I'm sorry but Room 12 is already taken," said Hannah. "But Room 9 has a fine view as well."
"Are you sure? We really wanted Room 12."
"Come and have a look," said Hannah and led them upstairs.

The geese liked Room 9.
"Good," said Hannah. "I'll get Rodney to
bring up your suitcases. Dinner is served from
eight o'clock." Hannah went back downstairs.

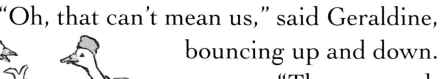

"Look, another notice,"
said Gillian. "It says
'Please don't bounce on the beds'."
"Oh, that can't mean us," said Geraldine,
bouncing up and down.
"They are such
bouncy beds!"

Downstairs, Hannah met Rodney
coming in through the front door.
"Ah, Rodney, would you
take these suitcases up to
– what's that, Rodney?"
"It's part of the
ferryboat engine."
"But Rodney, it's filthy."
"I know, that's why I'm going to wash it."
"But Rodney, not in the kitchen."
"Why not? I always used to
when your aunt was here."
"Well I think not, Rodney.
What would the guests say?"
At that moment Dora Dormouse passed by on
her way to the sitting room. She stopped and
looked at the engine.
"My word, a Gluck & Splutter Mk II. How
very interesting," she said and then tried
to get into the broom cupboard.

"That's the broom cupboard,
Dora," called Hannah.
"The sitting room is on the left."
Dora had been living at the hotel for
five years and always made the same mistake.
"Now Rodney, please take that round the back.
It's dripping oil on the carpet."
"Your aunt wouldn't have
minded," grumbled Rodney.

In the kitchen Sam
was unwrapping a parcel
of groceries. Everything
had its place in the kitchen.
Everything was labelled.
Sam put away the
strawberry jam
and plum chutney.
"There'll be two more
for dinner, Sam," said
Hannah, poking her
head round the door.
"So that'll be fourteen?"
asked Sam who wasn't
good at numbers.
"No, Sam, twelve."

"I wonder if I should make some
more soup," said Sam to himself.

Hannah left him to work it out.
Sam got flustered if there was anyone
else in the kitchen while he was cooking.

Hannah went into the office to type the menu for dinner. She'd just started when Geraldine and Gillian came downstairs in their bathing things.

"That Mr Mole in Room 12 is so nice," said Geraldine. "He let us look at the view. We thought we wouldn't really be disturbing him if we just had a quick look. And what a lovely view. There's, well, so much of it, isn't there Gillian, dear?"

"Ooo yes," said Gillian.
"He's an archaeologist,
you know. He digs up
things and he's writing
a book about it.
And guess what!

He's got a little blue suitcase just like ours!
He keeps important things in his.
So we said we had better not
get them mixed up,
had we? Ha, ha.
Well, we're off
for a paddle.
Bye, bye."

A little later Mortimer Mole came downstairs.
He looked rather upset.
"Is everything all right,
Mr Mole?" asked Hannah.
"Eh? What? No, it's not.
I told you I needed absolute quiet.
That I had to finish the book I was writing.
Well, although I put the
'Do Not Disturb' sign
on my door, two geese
just walked in wanting
to look at the view. The view! I ask you.
All they did was chatter non-stop.
Now I'm too upset to work."

"Oh, I'm so sorry, Mr Mole.
I quite thought you'd be
undisturbed at the top of the house."
"But what am I going to do?" said Mortimer.
Hannah thought for a bit. Then she noticed a
bunch of keys hanging by the door and she
had an idea.
"I know, come with me," said Hannah...

...and she took Mortimer Mole down to the cellar.

"Why this is perfect!" he exclaimed. "I can see I shall be quite at home here."

Hannah left Mr Mole hard at work.
She went back up the cellar steps and then
put a notice on the outside of the cellar door.
It read: 'Please Enter'.

Mortimer Mole didn't appear at dinner.
"I wonder where he can have got to,"
said Geraldine as the two geese
were studying the menu.

"Artichoke soup
would be nice," said Gillian.
"Parsnips don't agree with me."

Molly took their order.
"Two artichoke soups,"
she told Sam.
"We've run out of
artichoke soup," said Sam.
"There's only parsnip left."
    "Oh, parsnip will do instead," said Molly.
        "They won't know the difference."

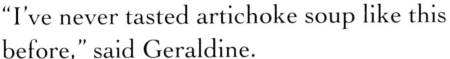

"I've never tasted artichoke soup like this
before," said Geraldine.
"Yes, it's delicious,
isn't it," said Gillian.
"I think I'll have
some more."

After dinner the geese looked about
for Mr Mole.

"Look, another notice," said Gillian when they
found the cellar door. "It says 'Please Enter'."
"Oh, we don't want to go in
there," said Geraldine.
So they didn't.

The two geese had a sleepless night.
"This bed is the most
uncomfortable I've
ever slept on,"
complained Geraldine.
"There seem to be
springs sticking out
all over the place."

"I don't feel at all well,"
said Gillian. "Perhaps
the artichoke soup
wasn't cooked
properly."

"This hotel isn't as nice as we thought,
is it Gillian, dear? I think we should
leave straight away."

Next morning Mortimer Mole was getting
ready to leave.

"I'm so glad you managed to finish your
book," said Hannah.

"Yes, I'm delighted," said Mortimer. "Now
where did I put my suitcase... I put it down
here a moment ago, I'm sure."

Molly came running
down the stairs.
"The geese left
in such a hurry
they forgot this!" she said.
It was a little blue suitcase.

"But they must have taken the wrong one,"
said Hannah.
"Oh, no!" cried Mortimer Mole in horror. "It's
got my book in it."
He dashed out of the hotel and almost bumped
into Rodney.

"Those silly geese have got stuck,"
said Rodney. "I told them they'd
have to wait for low tide
but they didn't listen.
Now I suppose
I'll have to rescue them.
As if I didn't have enough to do!"

But Geraldine and Gillian didn't wait to be rescued. They jumped into the sea and swam for it.

Dripping wet and dragging their suitcases, they struggled up the path from the beach.

"There should be a notice warning people of that," said Geraldine.
"We might have been swept out to sea."

"But my book! My book!" wailed Mortimer
Mole. He grabbed his suitcase from Gillian
and fumbled frantically with the catches.
"There's been a mistake –"
began Hannah but then
Mortimer Mole let out
a cry of despair.
The suitcase
was empty.

Then along came Dora Dormouse.
"Ah, there you are, Mortimer! I've been looking for you everywhere. I wanted to tell you how much I enjoyed this."
She was carrying a bundle of papers.

"Eh? What?" murmured Mortimer Mole.

"Your book," said Dora, "you lent it to me, remember?"

"Did I? – Oh, so I did!" cried Mortimer. "Hurray! So I did! I'd quite forgotten. Last night, before I went to bed. Thank goodness, it's safe after all."

Then the telephone started ringing. Molly went to answer it.

"Hannah," she called. "It's Mrs Gerbil. They're nearby and the whole family are coming across for a bit of lunch."

"Oh no," muttered Hannah. "Not the gerbils!"

Here are some more Picture Lions

BADGER'S PARTING GIFTS
Susan Varley

Quentin Blake
MISTER MAGNOLIA

KATIE MORAG AND THE TIRESOME TED
Mairi Hedderwick

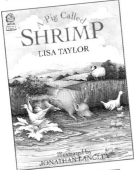

A Pig Called **SHRIMP**
LISA TAYLOR
Illustrated by JONATHAN LANGLEY

A BAD WEEK FOR ~ The ~ THREE BEARS
TONY BRADMAN & JENNY WILLIAMS

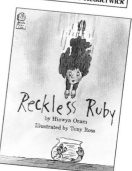

Reckless Ruby
by Hiawyn Oram
Illustrated by Tony Ross

Monsters
Colin & Jacqui Hawkins

WHERE THE WILD THINGS ARE
STORY AND PICTURES BY MAURICE SENDAK

Michael Rosen & Quentin Blake
DON'T Put Mustard in the Custard

for you to enjoy